Ellie
 I believe in the fairies
  Who make dreams come true
 I believe in the wonder
  the stars and the moon
 I believe in the magic
  from fairies above
 I believe in fairies that
  dance on the flowers and
  sing songs of love

Ellie I believe that you believe
 Please always stay true to the beautiful
girl you are.
  You have a heart of gold. And
 bring sunshine to all.

My dear granddaughter you always make
 me smile big when I am with you!
   I LOVE YOU BUNCHES Ellie

Hugs and kisses Always - Nana ♡

This book is dedicated to Andreas, whose vision and effort
made this book possible. His two nieces,
Zoe and Amanda, along with his nephew Spencer,
all helped discover the magic.

To my girls, who make every day magical.
Savannah, Sienna, McKenna and Ashtyn,
you are my world.

On a balmy Summer evening, a group of fairies flew over Laguna Beach, gazing down at the beauty of the ocean and sweeping canyons below. Fairy Lily, Queen of the Fairies, was mesmerized by the breathtaking canyons and fields of yellow wildflowers when suddenly, she felt a hard thump on her back. Her sister, Fairy Isabella Twilight, had accidentally run smack dab into her, knocking Fairy Lily in the back of her wings. Fairy Lily tried to fly straight again but she quickly realized that her wing had been injured. Lily struggled to fly with one wing, but couldn't.

She had to land, and of course, all of the fairies landed along with her. The fairies found themselves right in the middle of one of the most incredible places they had ever seen. Fairy Lily's Aunt, Fairy Cara Thistle Branch, known for her Compassion, immediately started tending to Fairy Lily's wing. After careful examination, Fairy Cara Thistle Branch realized that Fairy Lily's wing was broken!

The fairies got to work and began gathering small sticks and stones, twigs and leaves, anything they could use to begin building their temporary shelter for the night.

As dusk moved in over the canyon, Fairy Cara Thistle Branch finished bandaging Queen Lily's wing. The fairies knew that they had to prepare a place for her to get some rest. They gathered white sage, thistle and other natural plants to make a soothing balm for Queen Lily. After the fairies gathered soft grasses and many tender leaves, they built a large fairy nest for Lily to recover in.

That night, a beautiful sunset fell over the canyon in the shape of Queen Fairy Lily's wings, and the fairies knew that they would all be safe.

As Fairy Lily rested, the fairies gathered around the bonfire, and while roasting s'mores and drinking hot cocoa, they agreed that the canyon would make a wonderful home for several months, allowing ample time for Lily's wing to heal.

Fairy Isabella, the Fairy of Integrity, led the others in song and dance as they were all quite excited to have landed in this unique and beautiful place. They remarked about how they couldn't have chosen a more serene spot and it seemed to be fate to have this little unplanned vacation together.

Before they knew it, it was getting late, and a bit chilly out, so the fairies huddled close together and slept under the stars, counting more stars than they ever had before. They counted them softly until they fell asleep, vowing to count even more the next evening. Of course, they made their wishes upon the stars.

In the morning, to their delight, two mockingbirds began singing the most glorious melody, welcoming them to the canyon. Kindly, the mockingbirds brought them gifts of rocks and sticks so that the fairies could continue building their homes. The fairies named the sweet mockingbirds "Poppy" and "Feisty".

Later that afternoon, a beautiful group of hummingbirds came to visit the fairies, bringing them many types of flowers from the canyon and some twine. Fairy Catherine Apple Tree, known for promoting Citizenship, put a little bird feeder on her fairy home to reciprocate their kindness. She wanted to see them feeding outside her door and coming back regularly, too.

The fairies spent the next four days building homes for all twenty six fairies who now called Fairy Lane home for a bit.

They built the fairy homes with flowers, sticks, rocks, twigs and twine. Poppy and Feisty dubbed the fairies "The Caring Fairies" and the fairies loved the name so much that they decided to use it as the name for their group. They felt especially proud that the animals thought that they had virtues worthy of such a name!

Some days, Fairy Lily struggled to stay still so that her wing could heal. To help her through those tough days, her fairy friends would stop by to offer her snacks and entertain her with songs and dancing to keep her upbeat. Fairy Paloma Grace, known for Perseverance, told Lily stories of her time in Ireland and offered many stories of others who persevered to be "even better than before".

Fairy Ella Calypso, who stands for Empathy, shared stories in which she encouraged others to become more empathetic toward one another. She took note when she saw the fairies exhibiting even more empathy than they ever had and left them notes of appreciation along with small token gifts.

As The Caring Fairies relaxed and played in the canyon, they would often look out to the Pacific Ocean and squint their eyes to see dolphins frolicking in the Surf. The fairies wished that they could swim with them and get a little closer. They had never seen dolphins like these when they were in Ireland.

As the days went on, The Caring Fairies still couldn't believe their good fortune to have landed in such an amazing place, and named the spot "The Magical Trail", because it had a magical light and just being there seemed to bring out the best in all of them. The Caring Fairies began to hear footsteps on the trail almost every night and they were delighted to see such little beings trying to sneak a peek of them.
Since the fairies slept during the day and were awake at night, they didn't know that the little ones were also coming all day. Every once in awhile, they would look out to see a set of little eyes trying to peek in to catch a glimpse of them. The Caring Fairies were very shy so they quickly hid until the humans disappeared.

The fairies made many animal friends including crickets, tiny little mice, bunnies, squirrels, lizards and grasshoppers. You see, animals can see the fairies even when humans cannot. Humans who walked on the trail would often wonder why a dog would bark at the small homes on the trail. It was the dog's way of saying "Hello" and "Welcome" to the fairies who lived on The Magical Trail. Some animals even enjoyed chasing after the fairies.

One day, The Caring Fairies met two cute little squirrels and decided to name them as well, calling them "Sandy Cheeks" and "Peanut". The fairies built a chair for the squirrels to eat on while they took in the spectacular canyon views.

After Sandy Cheeks and Peanut finished eating, they would have fun chasing the fairies on the trail. Of course, the fairies delighted in these games because they could always get away by flying and using their magical powers or jumping on the back of the wings of their butterfly friends.

In the days that followed, The Caring Fairies began to hear more and more footsteps of little girls and boys walking around the homes they had built. They delighted in the trinkets that their human friends left for them and treasured the special notes that the children carefully placed at their door steps.

These jewels and flowers helped make the fairy homes feel even more special, and reminded them of their homes in Ireland. They giggled when they eavesdropped on the conversations of their new little friends and found themselves wondering what exactly they were talking about.

"Emojis" was a word they had never heard before and some kids talked about a game called Mining Craft or something like that. They were happy that the girls and boys enjoyed visiting them on the trail and overheard several parents remark that the kids had hiked "further than ever" while searching for more fairy homes. This, of course, encouraged them to keep building and building.

They often used the jewels the children left behind for a door handle on their homes and businesses. They stood back and admired the difference this made in their home's entrance. Sparkle makes everything prettier!

Each night, they continued to gather even more twigs, branches, rocks and jewels and would work together to build each other's homes, usually as a group because it was more fun to sing and be silly together.

After a month of building together, they counted the houses and discovered that they had 29 of them. There were colorful ones, big ones, small ones, wide ones, and skinny ones... They were so proud of their accomplishments. Fairy Ursula Sun, known for Unity, was especially ecstatic that the group had worked so well together to build such a stunning village. They even built a Castle for Queen Lily. Wow!

Lily, Queen of the Fairies, had an important position in the community. "Queen" represents the best in all of us. She's enchanted, helps everyone get along, promotes the fostering of friendships and helps all the other fairies see the very best in one another.

After the homes were completed, they built a Fairy Lending Library, including all the fairy classics...Tooth Fairy Stories: Volumes 1 through 10, The Art of Flying, Making Yourself Invisible, and Fairy Gardening. Reading was one of their very favorite activities as it helped them learn what other animals and people do.

They were elated to build a Fairy Wing Salon, where fairies could get fairy dust highlights on their wings, or rainbow coloring and sparkles! They giggled as they remarked that some of their friends back home in Ireland may not recognize them with their new "makeovers".

The Caring Fairies also built a special store for medicine, The Fairy Apothecary. It had potions and lotions to fix almost any ailment including one that seemed to help Queen Lily's wing heal. They called this one "Lily Balm" and even added some sparkles to it so she looked all sparkly when she applied it.

Fairy Francesca Star, known for Fairness, always made sure that all of the fairies had ointments and creams to keep them as healthy as could be. She left little packages on their doorsteps with notes detailing what she was "prescribing".

The Caring Fairies' community would not have been complete without Miss Sparrow's School for Fairies where young green wings (newborn fairies) learn to write letters in their very best fairy writing, how to paint flowers, make magic wishes, ride unicorns and chase fireflies, among other things. Fairies love to learn!

They also had tiny desks and lots of art supplies. Miss Sparrow allowed the fairies to paint the walls and their imaginations soared!

It turned out to be more beautiful than Miss Sparrow thought she could do herself. Many of the Fairies were named after character traits, which the fairies subtly encouraged others to develop.

Miss Sparrow loved to help the fairies come up with names for their little ones because she was a bit of a wordsmith.

For the grown-up fairies, Fairy Philomena's Coffee Shop served some of the very best imported Irish style coffee on the canyon. Fairy Shiloe Song, known for Self Control, worked at the shop and loved coming up with new blends like buttered popcorn and licorice. Fairy Renee Sea, known for promoting Respect, often helped her out when the lines were extra long.

They sometimes had "happy hour" and would offer special homemade treats like fairy ice cream, crispy treats, and handmade marshmallows shaped like their favorite little animals. Of course, they often brought these treats home to their children or invited them to enjoy the delights on the outdoor patio, where they played cards and board games for hours.

A spectacular addition was The Fairy Day Spa, for all fairies to enjoy, open from 1 AM - 3 AM. They had a little sauna, hot tub, and especially enjoyed the wing massages.

The Caring Fairies loved to play at night. The Fairies would tell tall tales to one another, paint flowers, and dance the night away. They even made their own musical instruments. Humans who lived in homes close to The Magical Trail reported that they heard the faint sounds of laughing and music at night.

One late night, they took a trip to see their dolphin friends and were over the moon when they saw the dolphins showing off and doing tricks for them. One dolphin jumped so high in the air that he was face to face with Fairy Shiloe Song and she sang out with delight. Fairy Sapphire Wish Seashell is a fairy who loved to go to the beach and bring back special shells to adorn the fairy homes. It reminded her of when her Mother would take her to play there when she was young.

Often they played their own instruments with their little cricket friends. They gave their cricket friends names like "Chirpet" and "Chancy" and helped them build their own cricket amphitheater.

The Caring Fairies also enjoyed playing peek a boo with the bunnies that lived along the trail. At first, they played with two sweet bunnies that they named "Silly" and "Smiles". Before long, Silly and Smiles brought their friends and they took turns hiding and finding The Caring Fairies. One night Smiles brought his brother, Flopsy, because he had injured his foot. The Fairies put a mini cast on his foot and brought him little treats while he rested. The fairies were kind enough to play near him so he could still be part of the fun and they knew that laughter would help Flopsy heal faster.

Fairy Lily loved hearing the stories of all her fairy friends. Many stories were about the magic that they spread to those along the trail. Even though she needed to rest in order to heal her broken wing, Fairy Lily couldn't resist listening to fairy tales and stories about places they could explore when her wing healed. Most of all, Lily liked to hear of all their nightly adventures and couldn't wait to join in.

Often, when Fairy Lily finally fell back into a light sleep, she would hear the other Fairies chanting her name and it made her giggle, knowing how much fun they were having.

As the months passed, The Caring Fairies saw that even more children were coming to visit their homes each day. The fairies created a fairy map to help the children find their homes.

Nights were always full of fun, and many fairies did not want to miss anything, so they made themselves "To Do" lists. In addition to adding special touches to their homes, some sang and danced, and others gardened in their yards. Residents even heard little footsteps as the fairies ran through the bushes, going from house to house. Always the planner, Fairy Candy Sparkle Sprinkle kept updating her "To Do" List to be sure that they didn't miss out on any fun.

The Fairies took turns telling stories of their adventures back in Ireland, usually one each night and then they would continue where they left off the next evening. When they were at home with their friends and family, they sometimes didn't take the time to nurture their special friendships as they did on The Magical Trail. They wondered why this was and vowed to take time out and smell the flowers more when they went back home.

Fairy Paloma Pea, another Fairy of Perseverance, told stories of how she persevered when she was stuck in a thunderstorm and was able to help others to safety. Fairy Beatrice Dahlia, the Fairy of Bravery, told stories of how she was not afraid to visit the home of the Wandering Troll who lived on the trail and she often brought him some berries and gifts, thinking that he may become nice if he was just treated gently.

Most all of the other fairies were afraid of the Wandering Troll that lived along the trail, but Fairy Beatrice Dahlia discovered that the troll was actually sweeter than anyone thought, even though he preferred to live by himself and didn't like to play with anyone. She spied on him and saw him doing kind things for others, but always anonymously. Fairy Beatrice Dahlia thought that he must have some anxiety about playing with others and felt sure that someday she would get him to join in their Fairy games.

The fairies had newfound respect for Beatrice Dahlia and praised her for being so brave and kind to the Troll. Fairy Ulrika Cherrypetals vowed to be like her the next time she got scared. Ulrika lives in the house that says "Dream" at the top, dreaming of a world where fairies, humans, trolls and animals can all live together in one place.

At the very top of the trail was a fairy lighthouse where a Gate Keeper, named Fairy Luna Starlight gave directions to others approaching the trail and checked to make sure that wandering trolls did not try to sneak in. The lighthouse had a super bright light in case the fairies got lost in the fog when coming home in the wee hours.

The Caring Fairies loved children so they were thrilled that one of the new homes was right near a kid's soccer field and they loved to sneak peeks at the children playing soccer. They even learned how to play a bit themselves and set up a little field of their own.

Fairy Serena Stargazer shared about Service to others and how good it feels to help those in need. Fairy Serena, who lives in a pretty little yellow house on the trail, helped The Caring Fairies find causes they could help with in the community while they were vacationing. She lives with her cousin, Fairy Francesca Forget-Me-Not, known for Fairness. Together they enjoyed helping others. They often visited children who were hurt, and used their magic fairy dust to help them heal faster. They would go to their homes at night and sprinkle their magic fairy dust all around them. They also searched for kids who felt alone, anxious or afraid and left them some things to lift their spirits.

Helping others together and doing kind things for others made them feel quite prideful. They vowed to continue to help others and have this kind of special camaraderie when they returned back to Ireland. They pondered whether they could have two homes; spending winter back in Ireland and Summers in Orange County and put it on the calendar of "things to discuss".

After four months of rest, Queen Fairy Lily's wing was completely healed and she even had time to do some fairy wing therapy to make her wing stronger than ever. One of the things she loved most was being able to play with her friends at the Fairy Playground, complete with swings, slides and see saws. She was amazed at all that her friends had accomplished while she was healing.

Every night, she joined in with the fairies who were dancing, delighted that she could now celebrate her good health again! Dancing and singing was their absolute favorite night time activity.

Despite having so much fun, they realized that they missed some of their friends and family back home. What was supposed to be a short trip had turned into quite a long one. They made plans to return to their home in Ireland on November 27th, 2017, the day before Thanksgiving.

They left notes on the doorsteps of their homes so that their human and animal friends would know of their imminent departure and could come say goodbye to them. They began to pack their bags, and gather the painted rocks left for them, as well as gifts and flowers that they wanted to take with them to remind them of special memories they would forever cherish.

They said their tearful goodbyes to Chirpet and Chancy, with promises to return someday. Poppy and Feisty brought the fairies special "lucky" feathers for their return trip. The morning the fairies were scheduled to leave, they were excited to see many of their human friends, both children and adults, wearing their own special fairy wings, bringing notes and farewell wishes for a safe journey home. They overheard them talking about how sad it was that the fairies would no longer be around.

"They really like us," The Caring Fairies said to one another! It was so touching and made the fairies feel very special. But alas, they knew that they needed to return home.

They cleaned up their homes and hid many of the houses up high in trees so that if they were lucky enough to come back someday in the future, they would not have to completely rebuild the homes. They certainly wanted to vacation in sunny California again and come back to paradise!

The Caring Fairies sprinkled fairy dust along the trail so that when the humans walked on it, they would know that the fairies wished them magic in every step they took! Saying goodbye is never easy but they tried to be strong, as they had a very long trip ahead of them and had to believe that they would see their human friends again.

The fairies were incredibly grateful for all the friendships they had made and vowed to cherish the trinkets and rocks their human friends had left them. They read and reread the special notes the children left behind for them. They even memorized some of them and would recite them whenever they wanted to feel love in their hearts.

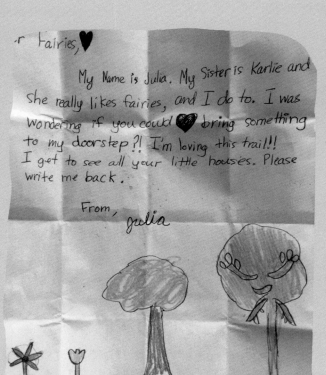

On the evening of their departure, a few people who remained on the trail reported seeing a super bright light in the sky, followed by a big flash. That may very well have been the fairies taking off.

Nearly a year later, after the fairies had enjoyed some time in Ireland reconnecting with their fairy family and friends there, they decided as a group that they wanted to head back to California. They wanted a place near the other trail but also wanted to have a new spot where they could build even more fairy homes, since they planned to bring a much larger group this trip.

Finally, Queen Lily, Fairy Shiloe Twinkle Sky, McKenna Rainbow, and Fairy Violet Starlight flew out ahead of the others to find the perfect spot and after looking for weeks, they were overjoyed to find the Oso Creek Trail in Mission Viejo. Fairy McKenna Rainbow, who stands for Morality, promised to call for the others back home when they found the perfect spot.

It had that magical light they were in search of, lots of huge trees and was very central to many places they wanted to visit at night. Fairies fly super fast and can cover tens of thousands of miles in a single evening.

They left a tiny door on one of the trees and built a very small home to wait for the others to come a few days after they sent word that they had found what was surely a very magical spot. They could hardly sleep while waiting for the others to come because they were so thrilled about their new location.

The fairies began to arrive to the Oso Creek Trail from Ireland in the morning hours before dawn on April 12th. The Owls on the trail were excited to witness their arrival, as they were up late. The owls helped them unpack their bags around the area of the park called The Enchanted Forest.

In the Enchanted Forest, fairies, unicorns and fireflies could all play together in a big grassy field by the creek. This particular trail had a maze and they had never seen one before. They had a ball getting lost in it and trying to find their way out. Of course, it was a perfect place for Hide-And-Seek.

31

In total, there were over 77 fairies that made the trip together including many new small fairy children who had never left home before!

The youngest fairies that made the trip were a set of triplets, only 22 months old and quite new to flying so they made some stops along the way. The little fairies were named Savannah, Sienna and Ashtyn. Their parents would let them choose their middle names when they were old enough to do so. The triplet fairies were "green wings", so naturally they started attending Miss Sparrow's newly constructed School for Fairies, where their skills grew each day.

Immediately, The Caring Fairies decided to build an enchanted village along the trail. Fairy Virginia Verbena built a fairy garden where all the fairies could grow beets, mushrooms, Brussels sprouts, and other vegetables to share with their animal friends. They had never had such a huge garden of herbs as they did at this new trail.

Fairy Maribeth Mimosa Featherdancer, the Matriarch to many, even built an art studio, so that fairies could create the most magical fairy paintings of their favorite butterflies, dragonflies and spiders. The fairies found that when they built more homes, more children would visit. This inspired them to work all night to make it better each day.

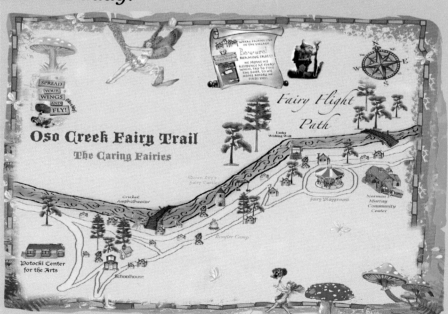

Some new animal friends came to welcome them. They created a resting spot for their frog friends from the creek and put a sign that read: "Frog Parking Only; All Others will be Toad."

Doggies from around Mission Viejo enjoyed talking to the fairies on their walks. One of their favorite doggy friends was Mia, a Maltese who loved to bring gifts to the fairies.

The sweet lizards loved to climb the fairy ladders and wait outside the fairy doors until they could come in for a snack.

 The fairies named two of their favorite lizard friends "Lizzie" and "Norman".

There were a lot of bunnies that loved to visit the fairies and bring gifts of carrots and celery for them at midnight.
One bunny, nicknamed Olean, short for Oleander, would always delight in coming to Queen Lily's Castle and bringing her special gifts. Although Olean could not come inside the castle because she was much too big, Lily would lay a picnic blanket outside her castle and invite Olean to share honey cakes and tea, together with other fairies. The Caring Fairies love their animal friends and always look for ways to help them.

LITTLE TOM'S HOUSE

Tom looks after the Fairy Trail,
he keeps it spick and span!

Because he was inspired by all the amazing homes, Fairy Tom Trillium built a larger home from rocks he gathered along the creek bed. Fairy Tom would wake up at night and tidy homes, tables, and stock the fire pit with logs for the bonfire at 1 AM, which earned him the nickname "Tidy Tom". Sometimes fairy homes were damaged by animals or visiting Trolls that were not so friendly. Fairy Tom, whose name stood for Tenacity, had the great ability to stick it out and never give up when repairing the homes.

At the Oso Creek Trail, the fairies discovered many human friends wanted to volunteer to help make the fairy homes extra special by adding little touches to them. The group called themselves "The Fairy Sweeper Brigade" and they helped Fairy Tom keep the fairy homes tidy so that when the fairies awoke at night, they would be surprised by new beautiful things. The fairies were so grateful for their support and could feel the love that went into their work.

Soon new fairies, previously unseen, appeared magically on the trail. One day, a Fairy Unicorn Home appeared, where fairies could meet at night to take Unicorn rides along the Oso Creek. At both trails, the kids loved to find the Fairy Castle, where Queen Fairy Lily lived with her two children and a housekeeper. The fairies had fun parties at the Fairy Castle and many performances. It was an ideal place to gather for events and big meetings because it held almost one hundred fairies.

The upper section of the trail was a wonderful place where Fairy Irene Daisy Starbutton, known for her Integrity, took the others to meditate and stretch. The Caring Fairies expressed their gratitude for their good fortune while they admired the views for miles.

Fairy Linda Apple Twinkle, known for her ability to spread Love to others, liked to stretch where there were a number of large pine trees, which provided a wonderful area to build mountain cottages. The fairies built Red Pine Hollow next to some pretty purple and green fairy cottages.

In order to get better cell service in the mountains, they even installed a Fairy Cell Phone Tower! It sure came in handy for reaching out to all of their friends and family back in Ireland.

Queen Lily loved to lead hikes along the fairy trail using the Fairy Map, even though she had it all memorized. She loved starting the hikes by stretching her wings, and then leading the fairies over the Troll Bridge, past the Snail Trail and heading down the trail toward the Plant Maze made of a huge hedge.

At the Plant Maze, the fairies loved to fly through the maze, chasing each other in a race with their animal friends. To their surprise, they were joined by Poppy and Feisty, their mockingbird friends from Laguna Beach!

No one knows for sure how long the fairies will be able to stay along the Oso Creek Trail, or how often they will return. But one thing we have learned about The Caring Fairies is that wherever they are, you can always find them by building a fairy home in your yard or home and writing a note asking them to come visit you.

Many boys and girls have reported that they could tell the fairies had visited because things were strewn about or jewels were left behind. As you know, they can magically fly at night from where they are to come visit you, their **very** special friend.

As you go to sleep tonight, remember to make a special wish on that twinkling star outside of your window, because it just may be your special fairy friends coming to dance, sing and play.

As Fairy Marigold Glimmer says,
"Always believe something wonderful is about to happen!"

Davida Mason, Andreas Frank and Kathy Kuiper

A very special thank you to ALL of the Volunteers and Fairy Trail Sweepers who help the fairies make repairs and keep the trail clean. A big shout out to Davida, who has been an extremely dedicated Volunteer on both trails and has a heart of gold!

Thank you to everyone who has donated to keep the fairy homes looking beautiful.

Donations are hugely appreciated and can be made directly on Fundly at:
https://fundly.com/support-the-caring-fairies-at-the-oso-creek-trail or
at www.thecaringfairies.com

Please "follow" the fairies on Facebook @ The Caring Fairies for updates on their adventures and travels, plus photos of the fairy homes.

Much Love, Queen Lily and all of The Caring Fairies

10360048R10031

Made in the USA
Lexington, KY
22 September 2018